Hold Still, Danny!

written and photographed
by
Mia Coulton

The little dog
is going to get a haircut.

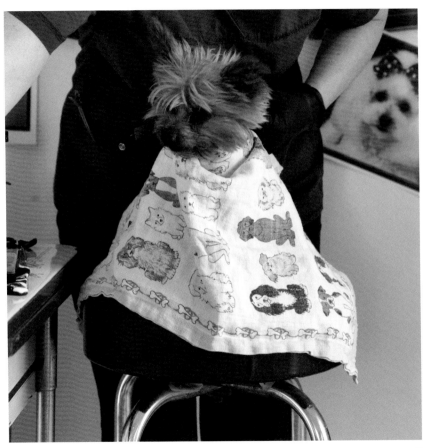

3

"Hold still,"
said the hairdresser.
"I am going to comb
your hair."

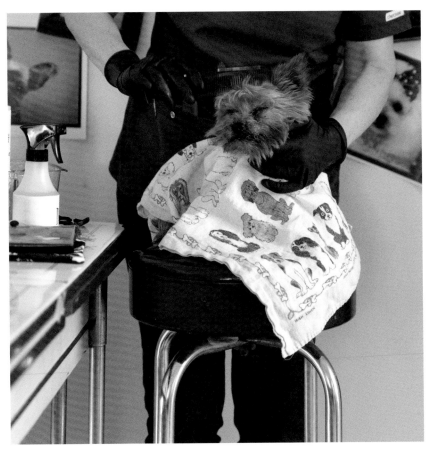

The little dog
did not want to hold still,
but he did.

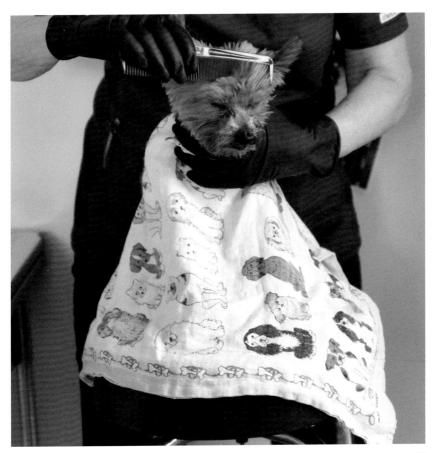

"Hold still!"

said the hairdresser.

"I am going

to cut your hair!"

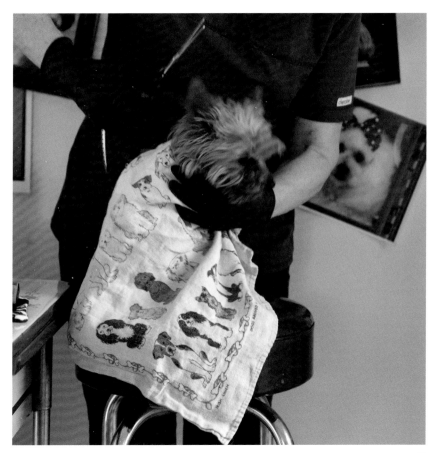

The little dog
did not want to hold still,
but he did.

"All   done,"

said   the   hairdresser.

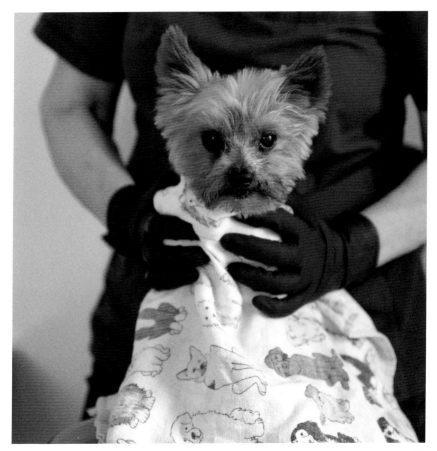

"Do you like your haircut?" asked the hairdresser.

"Who's next?"

"Hold   still,   Danny!"